I0624526

Muse
An Ekphrastic Trio

Muse
An Ekphrastic Trio

By

Michael Bloom

George Evans

David M. Hassler

 random acts books

Santa Fe, Indianapolis, Key West

Random Acts Books may be ordered through booksellers
or by contacting:

Random Acts Books
8 Paseo del Paloma
Santa Fe, NM 87506
randomactsbooks.com

Because of the dynamic nature of the Internet, any web addresses
or links contained in this book may have changed since publication
and may no longer be valid. The views expressed in this work are
solely those of the authors and do not necessarily reflect the views
of the publisher, and the publisher hereby disclaims any
responsibility for them.

ISBN-10: 0692411828
ISBN-13: 978-0692411827

Library of Congress Control Number: 2015936716
Random Acts Books, Santa Fe, New Mexico

First Edition: 3/20/2015

Praise For Muse

I know I like a story if I reach the conclusion and my attention lingers, wishing for just a few more pages, a few more words in a world where I've lost myself. All three stories in *Muse: An Ekphrastic Trio* inspire my yearning for an extended stay. The imagistic paragraphs of Michael Bloom's "Birth of a Folksong," haunt me with music, love and death in its pointillist mountain tale. The middle story, "Nighthawks," by George Evans, which is set in Edward Hopper's iconic diner, grounds itself with its narrator's vernacular soliloquy, letting us in on secrets under the fluorescents. And finally, there's David Hassler's "Aria," which is a gut punch with its crumbling relationship arranged artfully amidst Italian music, landscapes, and cuisine. With Hassler's flawed narrator, we taste every bite, hear every "Aria" note, feel every breeze. These three writers' moving ekphrases, fiction inspired by music and image, will arouse the reader's senses with their crafty yarns.

– Cate McGowan, author of *True Places Never Are*

This trio of stories, each inspired by a different work of art, will deliver you to the place where art is made and remind you, again, why art is essential.

– Barbara Shoup, author of *Looking For Jack Kerouac*

"Ekphrastic" is a literary device in which the author describes another work of art. It is also the basis for the premier publication of Random Acts Books–*Muse: An Ekphrastic Trio*. This trilogy of longish short stories showcases the work of Michael Bloom, George Evans, and David M. Hassler, and ekphrastic they are. Bloom's tale illuminates traditional folk music; Hassler mines the classical vein; and Evans, in an especially delightful turn, takes us within the frame of Edward Hopper's "Nighthawks." In geographic scope, the stories carry us from the mountains of Tennessee to New York City to rural Italy, and each author clearly knows his turf. Their prose sings (Hassler's "Aria" is especially layered), and their characters are wonderfully drawn: we meet lovers, connivers, and maybe even Humphrey Bogart and come away exhilarated from our encounters. This is what American writing should be: vibrant, urgent, often searing, and thoroughly compelling. You'll find yourself seeking out more of these authors' work. Yes, they're that good.

– Jerry Holt, author of *The Killing of Strangers*

Acknowledgements

We wish to express our gratitude to the hidden team behind this volume. First, to Steve Parolini, our editor, who told us only our words matter. Thank you, too, to Joan Kocak, whose photo provided the image for our cover. E molte grazie a Stefania Poli per fissare il mio italiano in "Aria." Finally, thank you to Ben Long, who created a marvelous cover for this edition that will be the foundation of a three-volume collection of tales tall, short and otherwise disposed. We'd also like to thank our very supportive–and very patient–spouses: Lisa Arthur, Karen Evans Moratz and Sarah Hassler. Here's to our own muses for their love and inspiration.

Contents

Birth of a Folksong
By Michael Bloom

Wake up, wake up Darlin' Corey . . .

In the breaking mist, on sodden ground, on half a ton of muscle and flesh, Patrick's legs wrap the stallion's girth. Shards of drizzled air spray against his face. Mud and leafage of the Tennessee mountains' McGilla Ridge coat the downside of rider and steed. Rumbling hooves, voices on the wind, echo from behind, muffled in dense spires of predawn fog. Riders closing in. Thieves, not of whiskey. Nay. The most hated and feared of all, who take what's yours and call it the law. Revenuers.

Patrick leans in, as if to whisper in the horse's ear. Faster, he urges, faster, swallowing the raging stench of damp hide. His heels dig into the horseflesh. Nostrils seething, the stallion charges, breaking through the bramble to the backside of a cabin, the home of Corey McGilla. He rears the horse up on its haunches bringing the beast to a sudden halt.

Leaping to the ground, he vaults up the two stairs and sweeps the backdoor open. The room, cold and damp, smells of ashen wood in a smoldering fire and the musk of spent seed. Who, he wonders, was it this time? Not that it matters. A far cry from his youth, from the scent of brewing rye whiskey and fresh goat stew in the afternoon. A lifetime from the starlit nights when she'd been his darling. Graying red locks poke from beneath the woolen blankets. He kneels beside the bed.

1

"Corey." He shakes her. "Wake up."

He needn't wonder what makes her sleep so sound. A whiskey jug, the best brew–her brew–lies sideways near his ankle.

The arrhythmic crash of hammers, steel on steel, rings dully through the twisted cracks of the cabin. Unrestrained voices shout. Revenuers found the still. Patrick draws a breath. Won't be long before they storm the cabin.

◆◆◆◆◆

A breath of June blew across the open meadow, a dry wind scented with brown grasses and the crisp, green pines and redwoods that ringed the untended clearing. Matthew Funicular rubbed the soft skin of the days-old blister on his right thumb, the blister he had gotten from Brianna. No. He had given it to himself. But she had pushed him to it.

He sat in the driver's seat of his faded bronze, seventy-four Dodge van in front of the mountain cabin above the dusty town of Othelo. He had chosen that place in the Northern California Mountains for its rare beauty and isolation. Angry silence bore down like a thick fog.

Box Valley was a study in contradictions. The mountain valley, with more square miles than the city of San Francisco, was discovered in the mid-nineteenth century by a pair of prospectors looking for gold. It became an Indian reservation with President Lincoln's signature just days before the fateful bullet blew his brains out. What had once been a holding ground for seven different tribes–only two of which were indigenous to the area–irrevocably transformed to a permanent home for all of them with a single flourish of the pen. And the town of Othelo sprang from the dry ground. Despite generations of intermarriages between the cowboys and the Native Americans, tensions still festered over land use, access and tribal rights.

Possession and birthright. The same issues that defined Matthew's relationship with Brianna.

The torn envelope from the San Francisco District Attorney lay on the passenger seat beneath the flyer for an upcoming rodeo, and a card from Mariel and Gabe, his children. Children he might never see again.

He picked up the card, inadvertently knocking the leaflet off the seat. It swooped down onto the top of the box with the gun inside, a replica of the long barreled, Remington forty-four caliber pistol, circa eighteen-sixties, that according to his research, Corey McGilla had carried. He had waited months for its arrival and picked it up days earlier in San Francisco. It was on that visit that he went to his apartment. Except that it wasn't his anymore, as Brianna had so invectively pointed out.

Her wicked wit, the acerbic voice that he had loved so much had, over the years, become vicious tirades, verbal stonings that she unleashed at him in any dispute. Lately, they had swelled to avalanches. The flame of love that once burned so bright had been devoured by its own passion until nothing remained but the arguments. And the anger–angry at her, angry at the system, angry at the world for being so unfair. Angry for letting it consume him and drive to this impasse.

Maybe Matthew shouldn't have pushed her against the wall, maybe he shouldn't have waved the pistol around, maybe he shouldn't have gone there without calling first, or even been there at all, as she had said. He just wanted the things he had been asking for. The things that were his.

Not entirely true. He wanted her, too.

A summer of misty daydreams and midnight love, strawberries and fresh cut flowers, a beautiful young art student from Dublin, the feisty Brianna. A just finished draft of his master's thesis, *Darling Corey: Birth of a Folksong,* a musicological analysis and history of the song, "Darlin' Corey." All that hope and fortune had disintegrated to a battle of wills, abrasive and lacerating to them all–Mariel and Gabe included. Nothing had worked out the way he had thought it would in the starry-eyed romance of his youth.

"The Housewife's Lament" had become his theme.

> *Oh, Life is a toil and love is a trouble,*
> *Beauty will fade and riches will flee,*
> *Pleasures will dwindle and prices will double,*
> *And nothing is as I would wish it to be.*

Matthew had dreams once, too. He'd brushed them aside to give Brianna the life she wanted, as a painter. He didn't regret it. What he did, he had done for love. He dropped the unopened card on his lap and picked up the torn envelope from the seat beside him.

Over the years, the arguments grew to daily feuds. Maybe he should have known when she suggested he take his sabbatical on his own. "To go as a family would be hard on the children," she'd said. "Where would they go to school? How would you get your writing done?" In the end, he had left–alone–with hope that in parting they would each find something of themselves again. That they would find their love again. His hope, anyway.

The manuscript was all he had left of his dreams. And even that she had tried to keep from him. He requested, asked and pleaded, demanded and insisted before finally losing patience.

Life is a toil and love is a trouble. Had he given up too much of what he wanted? In truth, he had done much better financially as a fireman than he would have as a professor. *Beauty will fade and riches will flee.* But in the end, had he really been able to afford the cost? It seemed a little late to ask the question now. Look how things had turned out for him. For them. Under any circumstance, going back was no longer an option. If it ever had been. *Pleasures will dwindle and prices will double.*

He had found himself knocking on her door, then pounding, then using the key she'd yet to demand back, for one reason only: to reclaim his property. He didn't go to snoop, steal or intimidate. But leave it to Brianna to twist things. Her specialty. Just when he had found what he'd been asking for, waiting for, looking for, Brianna walked in with the kids and some guy in tow.

And nothing is as I would wish it to be.

Matthew had been stunned. They were living separate but not separated. Not legally, anyway. What about the children? But she, as usual, had flipped out, burying him with her vilification. He reacted badly–but understandably–and pointed the unloaded pistol at the boyfriend. Pointing it, he had intended to be a joke. But cocking the hammer back? His thumb blistered with the ferocity of his rage. That was when she had grabbed the phone and dialed 911.

She had shrieked at him as he plodded down the stairs, blowing everything out of proportion, then threw his badly played banjo down behind him. Its neck snapped when it hit the bottom. And to think that she had once been his Darlin' Corey.

He thrust his hand into the top of the torn envelope to retrieve the offending document. His blister caught on a razor of paper and tore open again. Pain stabbed his thumb like a hot poker.

"Dammit."

He dropped the letter back on the seat and shook the aggrieved hand. No need to read it again. The words were etched in his mind with the acid of Brianna's hatred. "Civil Restraining Order." In short, he was barred from seeing or communicating with her or the children. Ever.

It wasn't right to keep a man from his son. How would Gabe grow up without him? Would someone else take his place? Matthew saw the frightened boyfriend's face. In his mind he pulled the trigger. Blood painted the man's forehead and spattered onto the wall behind him.

And Mariel. Would Matthew never see her bloom?

He picked up the card, gently tugged open the envelope. A family of stick figures on the front on the front of the card, drawn by Gabe, no doubt. Mariel's contribution scrawled on the inside: "We miss you, Daddy."

Matthew stared at the Mariel's words then closed the card. Gabe's stick figures gazed back at him. He opened and closed it several times, then set the card on top of the dash.

Brianna. How dare she?

His hand plunged into the open box and pulled the gun out then dove back in to retrieve the box of bullets. He jumped from the truck with the gun in one hand, ammo in the other and kicked the door with his foot. It creaked and slammed with a thud. Marching to the edge of the clearing, he drew six bullets from the box and dropped it on the dry dirt. He loaded the pistol, locked the cylinder in place and turned to the truck.

Eyes closed. Her face on the windshield. Fucking bitch. Keep me from my kids.

Eyes open. He raised the pistol and pulled the trigger. The gun's angry thunder echoed off the wooded mountain. The windshield crumpled just above the steering wheel, right where he had imagined her forehead, leaving a fractured hole with a spider web of cracks around it. An acrid sting brazed his nose. He bit his lower lip.

Restraining order. He lifted the weapon and fired again. The air cracked like the snap of a bullwhip. Another hole appeared in the windshield. A wisp of smoke floated past him. My kids, he thought, then shouted, "*My* kids." He fired again. He had a right to be angry. And again. It's fucking normal. And again. And again, until the windshield grew to a roadmap of bullet holes and sprawling cracks.

And nothing is as I would wish it to be.

Maybe this time Brianna had actually had the last word. Maybe not.

He squeezed the trigger. The hammer clicked on an empty cylinder. Matthew squatted in the dirt and counted out six more bullets.

◆◆◆◆◆

The revenue men are a comin' . . .

Corey's head pokes from under the blankets like a

waking turtle. The air wracks with the imperfect rhythm of hammers wailing on the still. She blinks a couple of time. Her eyes pop open wide, her lips tighten, her nose flares.

"The revenue men," Patrick says. "They've come to tear your still down."

Corey leaps from the bed, eyes sharp beads of anger. The wrinkles of age and hard living lay like a gauze of regret over the near-innocence and spirit he had once loved. As she slips on the dress lying atop the bed, he gazes at the five-string banjo hung on the wall above the mantel.

"Am I that hard to look at?" she asks.

Patrick's head snaps in surprise. "No, no. It's not that." He looks her in the eyes. "I just don't want to impose."

"Corey McGilla." A voice booms from out front.

"You best be going." She grabs the shotgun leaning against the foot of the bed.

"Corey?" Patrick steps toward her.

"Na-ah." She holds the weapon waist-high and cocks the hammers. "Nobody runs me off my land. Nobody."

"You can't." He steps up till double barrel brushes his midsection, then pushes it aside with a couple of fingers. "I promised your granddaddy I wouldn't let anything happen to you."

"He's long dead." Her thumb runs over the double hammers, releasing one then the other and lowers the weapon until the tips of the barrels hover just above the floor. "And you will be, too, if you don't get out of here."

"Corey McGilla," the voice outside shouts. "You are charged with tax evasion and selling liquor without a license. Stand forth and surrender yourself."

She slips a hand to the back of Patrick's neck and draws him closer. Vaulting on her toes she presses her lips against his. For one last time, he closes his arms around her and inhales her sweet, hot breath, the fruit of a passion that's never overripe, never past its prime.

Corey breaks their embrace and steps back. She takes her long barreled Remington forty-four with its bullet-laden belt from the chair beside her and tosses it to him. He plucks it from the air with a hand.

"You won't have a chance," he says.

"Patrick," she says softly. "Make me a song."

"Corey McGilla," the voice out front shouts. "Last warning. Surrender yourself."

"I'm coming out," she shouts over her shoulder, then whispers to Patrick, "Sing me something. Something you'll remember me by."

"Corey," Patrick pleads. "Don't do this. We can still get away."

"All I have," she spits, "is my still and my cabin." Then softly, "Besides, darlin'–I've been dead since you left me."

Patrick is stunned by the confession. Words stumble out of his mouth.

"You threw me out."

"And I'm doing it again." She blows a kiss that caresses his cheek but stings with sad fate. She whispers, "Make me one of your songs, Patrick."

The din of hammers permeates the air like dust on a mountain road under the full summer-moon. The world they know is quickly fading. Something potent and fierce is sprouting in its place. She's running from a future she can't– or won't–face. No good at compromise, he thinks. She never was; never will be. He breaks into a sad improvisation.

"*Wake up, wake up, Darlin' Corey. Whatever makes you slee-ep so sound?*"

She closes her eyes and answers in rhyme, "*The revenue men are a comin' . . .*"

Words spring from his mouth like whiskey from a broken barrel.

"*. . . For to tear your sti-ill house down.*"

By the time he finishes, she's heading out. Hinges creak as she steps through the door. It slaps the frame behind her, flapping a couple of times.

"I'm Corey McGilla." Her stubborn voice bounces off the surrounding hills. "Leave my still alone, if you know what's good for you."

Too late, Patrick thinks, for her. For any of us. He slips out the back and onto the horse. With his hands wrapped tightly around the mane, the steed drives through the bramble and brush, back into the trees of McGilla Ridge in the barely lifting fog.

"This ridge," Corey shouts, "has been in my family as long as anyone can remember. Now back up off my land."

Patrick digs his heels into the beast's gut, spurring it forward. Fingers of wind grip his face. A blast of the shotgun. Rider and steed are shrouded deep in the trees when thundering gunshots shatter the quiet beauty of McGilla Ridge.

◆◆◆◆◆

The moon glowed in the floor-to-ceiling window, above Matthew's reflection in the glass. His thumb ached dully. He sat motionless in the rocking chair with the card like a brick on his thigh. Gabe's picture scarred and discolored from the shattered glass, marred by layers torn from the surface, the edges shredded and bent.

Brianna. What a piece of work she had become. No. She was always a piece of work. He had loved that about her– until she turned on him. And what had he done? Given up his dreams for hers. Abandon his pursuits for her. And what had she given him in return? Wicked missives that tore his head from his heart. Wasn't he truly the victim? Whatever had happened, she brought on herself.

His fury had simmered and boiled throughout the course of the evening to the wee hours of the night. He didn't want the anger but didn't know how turn it off. Shooting out the windshield should have satisfied his rage. But it was starting to boil again. The angry smile glared from the window. A chill passed through him like a finger beckoning a forbidden passage. He turned away, fearing his reflection would reveal his darkest secrets, the ones he shuttered.

He lifted the shot glass from the floor beside him and sipped the Jack Daniel's, black label, glowering at the reflection. The gibbous moon peered into him from the night with invading eyes. Like Brianna's. Rage swelled. That bitch. What right did she have? Then despair. Gabe and Mariel. How could she? Then rage again.

He raised the gun with a throaty, "No," and pulled the trigger. Thunder in the small cabin. The glass crumpled to a waterfall of shards. A cool, night breeze swept in through the open portal, diffusing the cordite stench. Matthew gritted his teeth and pushed up out of the rocker, the pistol still gripped in his hand. The shot glass rolled, spilling the whiskey. He cranked his head and snarled once, then thumped across the floor through the empty window frame to the deck.

The blaze raging inside him flashed with each angry tally of his afflictions. Gabe, his only son. How dare she? He shot straight ahead, like Brianna stood not ten feet from him. Mariel, his sweet daughter. He fired down the mountain. And the moon. Brianna in effigy. He pulled the trigger with the barrel aimed high. An impotent display of indignation.

Wind brushed his face. The manuscript ruffled on the floor inside the mountain cabin. His wrath flared again, at the misery he had wrought to get his draft thesis, only to find it was nothing more than musings, a mockery of his aspirations. His life was no more than the ashen aftermath of a flame long since smothered.

He stomped into the cabin, grabbed the ream of paper from the floor by the rocker, then charged out to the deck. With a guttural roar, he heaved the manuscript into the night and shot at it. The bullet disappeared into the darkness, its report echoing off the mountain while pages fluttered down like glitter in the silvery moonlight.

He could shoot Brianna a thousand times and it wouldn't make any difference. Nothing he did ever had. Nothing ever would.

"Oh, fuck," he whispered.

The last pages danced into darkness. Matthew gritted his

teeth until his jaw ached and his vision swelled with tears. He cocked the hammer and raised the barrel to his temple.

◆◆◆◆◆

Patrick sits on the shore of McGilla Lake, sucking the hand rolled cigarette between his fingers. The rising sun filters through the morning fog, like angels coming for Corey. He blows a languid smoke ring.

'Twas there he first ever spied Corey. He, in the bushes at the edge of the trees, entranced by her music–that girl could play. She, thick waves of red hair halfway to her waist, long leather coat over her dress, hip boots like a second skin and a gun belt slung across her bosom–same one that lay in the wagon now beside her lifeless, bullet-ridden body. She hadn't been more than seventeen that day. Beautiful as the moon and fiery as the sun. In that moment, Patrick fell in love.

But she could be vicious as a coiled rattler, if provoked. Like yesterday. Her broken, bloody body paints itself on the inside of his closed eyelids. He shakes off the vision and fills his head with a memory of her some months back. Corey, with a dram glass full of trouble, some duster she'd picked up somewhere and a cold, hard smile. Not exactly the way he wants to remember her either. Patrick takes another drag off the cigarette and tosses the butt on the ground, spewing smoke and spitting out the image with a sliver of tobacco.

"Guess it's time to get going," he says to no one.

He grabs the shovel from the repurposed whiskey delivery wagon. At least the government thieves had allowed him to give her a decent burial. He plods to the water's edge and sinks the spade into the dirt here, then there, until he chooses the spot to lay her to rest.

Marking the ground with a dotted line of slices with the shovel, he digs into the dirt and tosses it to his side. He digs in again and again until the ground before him starts to recede and the pile beside him grows to a mound. A glint of sunlight reflects on the lake. The day is warming. At least, he thinks, she'll have good weather for her ride to heaven. If that's where she's going.

He hums the tune he sang with her in the cabin while he scoops the dirt onto the pile beside him. No words, just a forlorn melody. He hums faster, keeping time with his digging. Words form in his mind and he sings, a lone voice mourning in the wilderness, smoothing the way for to send Corey home.

> *Dig a hole, dig a hole in the meadow,*
> *A hole in the cold, cold ground.*
> *Dig a hole, dig a hole in the meadow,*
> *For to lay Darlin' Corey down.*

Darling Corey: Birth of a Folksong
by Matthew Funicular

Nighthawks
By George Evans

They call it Mulry Square like it's some kind of special place. It ain't. I'll give youse that maybe it *was* something, maybe back when the diner was there and times were different. Some pretty famous people thought so, anyway. Painters. Poets. Writers. You know, your artsy and your fartsy Village crowd. But come on. Now? Give me a break.

All that was way back before they called it Mulry Square. Tell you what, bet youse a Nathan's that you wouldn't find old Ed Hopper looking at the place today and thinking about painting those "nighthawks" of his. Not with the place like it is these days, no way in heck. Times change, as they say. And often as not, not for the better. I knew him by the way, that Ed Hopper. "Eddie" he let me call him, like I was somebody. Eddie. Ain't that something?

Anyways, these days, Mulry it's owned by the Transit Authority; just another empty lot sitting there as oblivious as I would be sitting around on some trading floor down Wall Street amidst a world of ruckus and flying paper. I watched the lot empty out over the years, so I should know. Lived across from the place longer than I'll admit to. I'm talking way back to when I worked The Boulevard Diner that used to be smack dab in the middle of it. Back in the late 30's and 40's it was, on up until some big wig bought her, used her up and said "see youse" like she was your basic peep show stripper getting the heave-ho after some up close bumping and grinding, if you know what I'm saying.

All gussied up she was back then, her new-fangled fluorescent glow buzzing like Mademoiselle Chanel all night long, the "Phillies Cigars 5 Cents" sign lit at 8:00 PM, extinguished at 6:00 AM. And talk about some damn good coffee. I should know, used to make it myself. Chock Full o'Nuts. Heavenly coffee. Delivered by Mr. buck-shoed Billy Black himself once a week as regular as a morning constitutional on account of some relations with the owner or the owner's wife. Never did find out the particulars.

All I know is, The Boulevard Diner was the only place in all of New York where you could get Chock Full o'Nuts outside of one of Billy's own nut shops, so I'm telling you, there was something going on with that. I'd bet my hat on it. Where there's smoke there's somebody cooking something, you know what I'm saying?

Nowadays, well, Mulry it's still sitting there right "where two streets meet," as Eddie was fond of saying; only now they're two streets all covered in all manner of this and that with folks going loudly here and there in a bray of car horns and the whole corner smelling like car exhaust or pee, depending upon which way the wind's blowing. Don't know how else to put it. I'm too old to be casting aspersions and too stupid to be offering explanations–I call them like I see them.

Anyways, Eddie Hopper's nighthawks, they still wander through and past to this very day, heading up Greenwich Avenue and stopping to relieve themselves in the square. Nighthawks, Eddie called them. Lost souls if you ask me, God bless them every one. They wander up and basically Mulry is their *pisserie* as we used to call it back in the day as in, "I shall retire to the pisserie, get me another Reingolds, would you kindly my good man?" You know, putting on airs, like.

So they come. They go. Up Seventh Avenue. Back down Seventh Avenue. Same with the ones out Eleventh, past the church. All who wander are not lost? Baloney, basically. Lost is lost. And folks, they don't pay much attention to the lost other than maybe tossing them two bits or so, no doubt warding off guilt and any worry that they'll wind up like that themselves one of these days. Who knows? Like I said, can't speak for other folks and their charity or lack thereof. Let he who is without sin, you know, not cast rocks asunder or whatever.

So yeah, Eddie's nighthawks, they head back down here eventually and do their business behind the storage shed the Public Works put up. Pretty much, that's the only monument to pretty much anything you'll find in Mulry Square these days. Public Works. You'd cry if you don't laugh, it's such a far cry from when Pee Wee Reese or Arky Vaughan would come by for coffee.

A lot of them Dodgers would come up after a night of it, dodging the streetcars on their ways home, uptown. The coffee was that good, I'm telling you. Yes sir, those Dodgers liked their coffee, all right. Schoolboy Rowe. Cliff Dapper. Frenchy Bordagaray. Dixie Walker, the bum. Come in they would, raucous as a foul tip, and take over the joint. Won 104 games that year. Lost 50. Brought a cattle smell with them: grass and sweat and meat. Leo Durocher himself came in one night. Had five cups of heavenly coffee, three sugars, ate six crullers and went to the pisserie at least five times, no kidding. What can I tell you–he did things his own way, that one. Died the same way, too. Natural causes, they said. Three sugars and six crullers times 86 years, I say.

Anyways, my point is, like a lot of things, what they call Mulry Square–all of this–is very different from back then. And like I was saying, it ain't necessarily changed for the better. The storefronts are gone. The ones that aren't boarded up, they got metal shutters to keep out the riff and the raff. Pawn shops, mostly; electronics and geegaws mostly; run by dark-skinned guys with names like Rastegar and Patel. Hey, live and let live I say.

Where maybe you once would have smelled liver and onions frying over to the Limey's or garlic and olive oil cooking on account of some Wop instigating a marinara, now it's all bloody and ripe and gamey smelling, like the pens over

to the Bronx zoo. Or the '42 Dodgers. An affront to the old
schnozz, I'll tell youse, though I have developed a taste for
cardamom in my coffee. Go figure that one on your abacus,
why don't you?

And another thing, where once you would have heard
Benny Goodman coming out an open window or three—or
Artie Shaw or Peggy Lee sounding like an angel from
heaven—now its banging and boinging and a backwards kind
of wailing all sounding like some poor schmucks just missed
on the trifecta out Belmont. Haven't acquired a taste for that,
no sir. Give me *Jersey Bounce* any day of the week.

Anyways, back to my story—the one Eddie made famous
here after that night, the heart of which is how some things,
well, they don't change. For better or worse. When it comes
to Eddie's nighthawks, what you have to realize, see, is that
the world's always had 'em. Mulry Square's always had 'em,
like they're drawn to the place like flies or prodigal children,
both in good times and in bad. Take you, for instance. You're
here, now, ain't youse? See? See what I mean?

Hell's bells, even when I was working the diner and the
place was a sight spiffier, I seen plenty of them. And I'm here
to tell you that I know for a fact that that's what Eddie was
getting at in that famous painting of his. He never let on
mind you, even after he went big time. No, he'd sit and drink
his coffee—put a little somethin' somethin' in it from this old
silver flask of his, if you know what I'm saying. He'd just kind
of take things in without really ever saying much besides
please and thank you, never letting on no matter how many
people asked him. "It's a painting about where two streets
meet," is all he would say. Polite enough, for sure, but all
enigmatical with that little grin letting folks know there was
more to it but he wasn't copping to it.

Left a lot of folks wondering in the end, those artsy fartsy
types. But not me, no sir. What's more, I was only happy to
tell pretty much anyone who'd listen and maybe buy me a cup
of coffee or slip me some loose change. Yes sir, I chronicled
it for folks time and again from right over there behind the

counter, like I was the goddamn librarian of Greenwich Avenue. I know the story because, friend, I am the story.

Trust me, you can see the whole thing for yourself in that painting of his if you have a notion and take the time. Eddie got it right and he got it straight from the horse's mouth, right there at that same counter day after it happened. And I'm tickled as Sally Rand that he also got rightly famous for it. The boy had talent. Got the whole thing pictured right down to the butler door that led to the back hall where we had ourselves a proper flush toilet. The *pisserie*. I told him my story and he soaked it all in so that when he told it himself in that old painting of his it was like he'd been sitting there at the counter himself the evening his nighthawks came in the joint and stirred things up.

Anyways, it was a dark and stormy night! Actually, it wasn't, really, I just like to give it a sense of the dramatical is all. So this pair comes in. Her I notice right off the bat and you would have too, let me tell you. She was a real looker. Hadn't been sent akimbo like that since the first time I saw Seabiscuit on the actual hoof. I'm talking hubba hubba, if you know what I'm saying.

So I tip my piss cutter. You would have, too. Long curly red hair she had, a regular three-alarm shine to it, too, you know, courtesy of them new fluorescents. Man, those babies didn't let you miss a trick, those things. Even redder dress, short sleeves, front cut wide and low off the shoulders so you can see her collar bones and more if you'd have cared to take a sneak peek–if you were less a gentleman than say me, for instance. Ok, so maybe I did take a peek bending down to finagle a cup and saucer and then a spoon and then a napkin and then another spoon. You'd a done the same if you had reconnoitered a gander down the front of that dress and don't you tell me any different.

Anyways, she kind of has this Joan Crawford kind of puss on her like she could show you how much she loved you and hated you both in the same expression. Cat crazy, my Ma used to call that look. So she orders a coffee, extra cream and extra sugar, and she keeps checking her nails like she's expecting one to chip right before her very eyes, or maybe like one already had for some reason like maybe she scratched a guy. Red as Stalin, I remember thinking at the time. And cut you just as quick. No wedding band I notice. Girl like that, you look, let me tell you. A girl like that you notice.

Him I don't remember so much mostly because I was fixated on his hat, an out-of-style Al Capone number. Plus some folks, no matter what, are pretty much just unremarkable, if you know what I mean. I have this fuzzy picture of him: kind of a quiet, faceless guy who parks himself one stool off the corner. And I only remember that because it was where Leo Durocher sat that one time, killing himself with crullers.

Anyways, I pour the Capone guy a cup of Chock Full o'Nuts, and as I sit here now, I can't remember for the life of me how he takes it. Ain't that funny? Not laugh-out-loud funny but ironic funny, like a catfish. Let's assume he takes it black for the purposes of my story. Anyways, I'm sure it's a cup of Joe, because he throws the damn thing later on.

So they're sitting there, him sipping away like the coffee is too hot, which it ain't, and her checking her nails. I'm pretty sure he lights himself a cigarette, they all did back those days before it bothered folks so much and before they invented cancer. But what strikes me most is the way they aren't talking and you can't help but notice something like that or wonder why. No scratches on the guy so that ain't it. Just, you know, curious, is what I'm saying.

I do pour him a refill after awhile without him asking; I always do that with everyone. Professional like. "On me," I say by way of pleasantry. And boy did I get that part right, but I'm getting ahead of myself.

Anyways, this other guy comes in and sidles his way around the pair and back to the far corner. The guy looks just like Bogie—just like him! I remember because I had just seen The Maltese Falcon again. It was playing special in a double feature with Casablanca, which was still showing, believe it or not, over at the Jew cinema in Crown Heights.

Anyways, this guy, like I said, is the spitting image. Eyes like sunny-side-up eggs. Fedora–a beauty, let me tell you– dimpled perfect, black band, pushed back Bogie-style on his head. Blue shirt, I remember that, don't ask my why. Dark tie. Padded shoulders making him bigger than life. Shirt poking perfectly out the sleeve–we're talking some tailoring, something you see a lot of, both good and bad working a counter let me tell you. Lean in, you can tell he overdid the Pontevecchio, but whose counting? Anyway, this guy has Bogie written all over him. I pour him some heavenly coffee, making it snappy. A guy like that, you make things snappy for.

"Got a light?" he asks. Won't lie to you, only place he could possibly sound like Bogie would have been in my imagination because you can't miss the Brooklyn in it. Of all the coffee shops in all the boroughs of all of New York, he's got to walk into mine, get it?

Anyways, he's not sitting there thirty seconds, no kidding, and Joan Crawford's up from her stool with her coffee in hand walking back around toward the *pisserie* only instead of going out back, down she sits right next to Bogie. Right next to him. Just like that. And still nobody says nothing. Not Bogie. Not Joan Crawford. Not Al Capone.

I look from one to the other to the other. Capone's kind of hugging himself, looking down like he's thinking about something thought worthy. She's back to checking her nails. Bogie's looking at me all Bogie smug like strange dames sit down next to him on a regular basis. And then there's me, looking back at him with this dumbass look on my puss–like he's the cat's whiskers and I'm just a dumbass.

That's when I reach under the counter to turn on the radio I have hid there, you know, for times like that when I need a little music to maybe liven up the joint. Something snappy, maybe. You know, music to sooth the savage breast or whatever. Just something at that point. Anything, really.

Point is, if youse were to pop a picture of that exact

moment–freeze it like the picture of the flag on Iwo Jima or the one of that sailor kissing that nurse dame in Times Square on VJ day–that right there's the picture old Eddie took from my storytelling and made famous. Yes sir, he snapped it up from my tale 'o woe like he'd been sitting there himself, the whole damn time.

Anyways, what he doesn't show you is what commences from there, which I guess would have been hard given the circumstance. Though with his take, he leaves you to ponder what's happening and what happens next and maybe that's the allure of his painting after all. Maybe that's the point. Because what happens next is that Capone's coffee goes flying like one of those Jap zeros we'd been hearing about coming out of Midway. Chock Full o'Nuts all over the back wall and the *pisserie* door. Chock full 'o pissed off, I might add. Then Capone up and leaves just like that. No gunplay. No guff, like you'd maybe expect if some guy some way shape or form moved in on your dame. I look at Bogie. I look at Joan Crawford and her sourpuss face. She shrugs and goes back to pondering her nails. Bogie raises his cup to me and nods and takes a sip like it's nothing, just exactly like you'd expect from Bogie.

"Good coffee," is all he says. Wow, can you imagine?

I dab some that splattered off my sleeve and all I can muster by way of a reply is that same dumbass look. I mean, what's a guy to say?

So I just get to cleaning up. Nobody says nothing else, like to them this sort of thing happens all the time. And I certainly ain't got nothing to add to the discussion. So I don't. They leave together and all of a sudden I'm wanting the radio louder for some reason. Something familiar, you know? The way the right tune at the right time can set you on an evener keel and such? How do you show that in a painting? You can't that's how. Just my luck, there's no Jimmy Dorsey. No Les Brown or Sammy Kaye. No Art Mooney or Glen Gray even, and I sure as shootin' could have used some *No Name Jive* at that point, let me tell youse.

No sirree Bob, it's all Japs, more Japs and more bad news all up and down the dial. I'm just hoping for a break, is what I'm saying and all I get is poor, poor grieving Clark Gable–it's been a year, c'mon–and Eddie O'Hare getting shot down and some nightclub fire over to Boston and war bonds and on and on and on. Hell's bells, at that point, I would have settled for some gassy old Guy Lombardo, but like I said, no such luck. Sorry, I'm getting away from myself. Can't help it sometimes, you know, the way a good song can make everything all hunky dory?

Anyways, by then it's getting to be closing time and I tell myself to stop going on about it. And I don't think about it much again, really, until me and old Eddie got to talking about it that fateful day, him sitting there at my counter intent on listening and me intent on running my mouth.

In the end, I worked that counter either full time or part time off and on until the establishment leveled her, like I said, back in '74. Watched it from across the street as they took her out top down, first with the Phillies Cigars sign, then the windows Eddie-boy made famous and finally the rest of her, gone in one fell wrecking-ball swoop like a cup of coffee what got side-armed against a wall.

But all them nighthawks? Let me tell you, they just kept coming, like damned pigeons, homing in to Mulry Square. And they keep coming, to this very day. They make their place here and they make their peace here–and they make their piss here. As do I. As do I, out back by what used to be the *pisserie*, back behind the Public Works shed, like I was saying earlier.

No regrets though, I'm practically immortal thanks to Eddie and that famous painting of his. He had a talent, boy. A real talent. He got the story down near to perfect, just like I told it to him. Right down to the door to the *pisserie* and right down to that red dress. Even the dumbass look on my face. Right up until...

Others, they all tried to capture my story over the years, bless their hearts. Talked to a good many, too–the painters, poets, the writers–they sought me out special. Me! Can you imagine? Joyce Carol Oates, even, that one time. Kissed me on the nose and then wrote a poem about it. The painting, not my nose.

One guy–this Kraut painter, Gottfried von something or other–he took me literal and got it pretty darn close, but with James Dean and Marilyn Monroe instead of Al Capone and Joan Crawford. But Bogie's there, all right. Even made old dumbass me in his version of things into none other than Elvis Presley. The King! Can you imagine that? Nice enough fellow, too, for a guy I could've just as easily been shooting at one time or another but for my flat feet.

Anyways, that's the real story of it sure as I'm telling it to youse. And, Lord willing, I hope to keep on telling it to good folks like you for a good long time. Well, for as long as folks are willing to listen, anyways.

Oh well, as old Bosko used to say long before that Porky Pig fellow coined the phrase: "tttttthat's all folks."

Now, friend, if you could just spare a fin for a cup of coffee, I'll let you on your merry way. A fin. A fin! Can you believe it? And the coffee, it ain't nearly as good as it used to be. Not by a long stretch. Not by a long stretch. Still, as long as it's hot, I'll take it and be thankful, because hot is good and a guy like me he needs that. Maybe add a little somethin' somethin." You know, to maybe warm up the story telling'? A little cardamom would be nice, too, thank you very much, like the locals do it nowadays. Odd I know. But, these days, hells bells, what ain't?

Aria

By David M. Hassler

Recondita armonia

di bellezze diverse!

È bruna Floria,

l'ardente amante mia

-Cavaradossi

TOSCA, Atto primo.

Giaccomo Puccini

Sometimes it's a new recording of *Tosca* with an extra thrust of longing in the first upward swoop in Cavaradossi's Act One aria, the one where the tenor sings of his ardent love for the dark Floria Tosca even as he paints a loving portrait of his blond patroness. Other times, it's the scent of roasted garlic or the freshest basil, maybe a sauce with the perfect hint of saffron. Or even just the words printed on the menu at Primi Piatti, the latest favorite of DC's journalists: *Risotto ai fiori di zucca al prosecco*.

For the next hour, my lunch companions will likely wonder at my distraction, my haste to finish the meal even as I savor the zucchini blossoms, my lack of attention to the latest innuendo over Clinton's impeachment and our continuing scorn at his failure of discernment in just who he allowed to suck his Presidential cock. They might even ask after my health and, leaning forward slightly, a certain look in their eyes, of how things were with Karen and me. "Fine," I might say, "just fine." Not exactly typical for the *Post's* classical music critic and noted reviewer for *Fanfare*, a man often chided not only for his barbs but also for his magnificent verbosity.

But I know I'm lost. I long to return to the Nixon years and a grad school orchestra tour and an Italian village on the plunging shores of Lago di Como. I daydream the narrow Alpine lake again, the scarps overlooking the churning water, and the villages rappelling down to the shoreline. Varenna, with its unexpected palms and those tall slender cypresses that shout of Italy. With its stunning palette of ancient buildings in every hue of bisque and tangerine, paprika and apricot, even pomegranate. I yearn for solitude so I can yield to another old story, close my eyes, and seek those lilting voices to see if they still puzzle and beguile after more than two decades. I imagine that perfect risotto with its satin texture and the secret of its floral magic. I even dream Karen with a fading echo of her sweetness.

◆◆◆◆◆

"Where's the green peppers?" Karen swept her risotto around the plate, then clattered the fork onto the deep blue china and sat back from the table. "This is *not* what I ordered."

"But it's . . . " Paul glanced around the restaurant. Through the high arched windows overlooking Lago di Como, the slant of evening sunlight burnished the amber walls and azure tablecloths and cast an elaborate web of shadows across the slate floor tiles. The staff and guests in hushed conversation, the muted clink of silver against plates, and the aromas of garlic and saffron. And, just before she turned from our table, the dark eyes of the teenaged girl who filled their water glasses. Long, long hair, so dark and smooth, glossy as a Steinway. When she reached the kitchen door, she looked over her shoulder, caught Paul watching, smiled and tossed her hair, then disappeared.

And then Karen's own look skewered him, a firming of her lips, something muttered under her breath.

"It looks delicious, Hon." He reached across the table to sample her risotto. She wouldn't look at him. Savory, the tang of *burro acido*, the *riso* stirred lovingly to al dente with the final ladle of prosecco absorbed to perfection, the Parmigiano-Reggiano fresh and nutty, a scattering of fresh basil. Sheer delight. "What's wrong with it?"

"I can't eat this." She perched her handbag on the table and rummaged through it with both hands, as if she'd lost something priceless. "I wanted that whatever flower special."

"*Fiori di zucca*, the zucchini blossoms."

She sat back and lit a cigarette, "Yeah, right, I bet they were out of it just for us Americans." Blew the smoke toward the ceiling. "Show me a single goddamn pepper."

"But you ordered," Paul gestured over his plate as if conducting a diminuendo. "Risotto *al pepe verde*, green peppercorns. Not peppers." But in his brief disappearance with that Julia the previous night at the chamber orchestra festival in Lindau, he'd squandered his store of leverage. All day, Karen had dragged him through purgatory—sitting in silence against the window on the tour bus, pointedly not touching him as they climbed from the Bodensee into the alps; avoiding his solicitous questions through an alfresco lunch with most of the string section in a rippling meadow above St. Moritz; and ignoring him entirely during their brief rehearsal for tomorrow evening's concert on Varenna's cobbled piazza in front of the church of San Giorgio. Step lightly. "Here, take this one, the saffron." Paul held out his plate for her. "It's deli—"

"I wanted green peppers and—waiter, *ragazzo*." She waved her cigarette in the air. "Come here."

"It's *cameriere*—'waiter,'" he put his plate down and tried to touch her hand. "*Ragazzo* means 'boy.'"

The waiter floated past.

Karen took a long draw on her cigarette, looked everywhere but his way.

When the waiter returned, Paul tried again. "*Mi scusi, cameriere.*"

The waiter slowed, half turned toward us as if his inertia were too great to overcome. "*Sì?*"

"*Mi dispiace*, but," Paul pointed to Karen's risotto, searched for the right words. "I'm sorry . . . *lei vuole un diverso . . .*"

"*C'è qualcosa che non va?*" At last the man came to a stop.

"No, no, nothing's wrong. *Niente.*"

"*Bene.*" He turned to go.

"Damn it." Karen grabbed the waiter's arm.

The waiter flinched and swung around, scowled at her. "*Che cosa?*"

"I can't eat this."

"*Che c'è?*" He glanced at Paul.

She waved her cigarette over the table as if casting some spiteful blessing, then loaded her fork and dribbled the risotto onto the plate. "It's full of peppercorns."

The waiter laughed. "Of course it is." He turned to go. "*Sciocca donna americana.*"

Karen stared at Paul. "And you sit there and do nothing?"

"But sweetheart, he's right—I mean about the risotto—"

"Don't 'sweetheart' me." She leaned toward me. "He just insulted me and you don't give a crap?"

"Karen, I really . . . "

"Maybe if it had been that little blonde cellist of yours," she grabbed her napkin and wiped her mouth. "That Julie."

"Julia." Shit. "Come on, honey, not a thing happened with her." That single kiss.

"A lot can happen in an hour."

"But nothing—"

"Especially with you."

"Damn it, Karen, I've already forgotten her and Julliard's off on their own tour who knows where." Vienna, then Prague. "She has a boyfriend, anyway." Jesus. Paul glanced around the dining room, caught once again the dark gaze from the girl who'd reappeared at the kitchen door. She didn't look away. Maybe fifteen . . . sixteen? He couldn't help a brief smile. "Karen, I'm," he finally looked back across the table. "We've got six more weeks on this tour before fall semester, and I really don't want—"

"*You* don't want?" She took another drag on her cigarette, closed her eyes. "What about what I might—"

"*Scusi.*" A woman stood over the table. "*C'è qualche problema?*"

"*Nessun problema. Mi dispiace.*" What was the word for misunderstanding?

Her eyes glittered with anger. She must have been in her late forties, an archetype of the Italian matron, buxom yet well balanced, her dress in a deep violet frescoed with petite flowers in cream. Her fingers played a cadenza over a handful of the hundred tiny buttons snaking up the front, tracing her curves. Hair and eyes equally black and glowing. Those same dark eyes. That same hair, kissed with gray at the temples. Paul glanced toward the kitchen. The girl had disappeared.

"I got the wrong dish." Karen simpered at the woman. "All I wanted was green peppers since you somehow were out of the zucchini blossoms. Are you the manager?"

"*Sono la proprietaria.*" The woman's chin lifted slightly. "*Il mia risotto al pepe verde è perfetto.*"

Karen looked at Paul.

"She's the owner and—"

"I get what she said." Karen waved her cigarette at the woman. "I need to speak to your husband."

"*Non sono sposato.*" The owner narrowed her eyes. "*Sono l'unica propriataria.*"

"She says she's not married and—"

"Yeah, right, but what are you going to do to get me a decent dinner?"

Small victories, he figured. "Do you know what you want?"

"I *wanted* zucchini blossoms and had to settle for green peppers. And even that was screwed up. The menu should be—"

"*Non ho peperoni verdi.*" The woman looked from Karen to

Paul, took a deep breath, and at last gave a slight smile. "*Cosa vorrebbe invece?*"

"I don't want something *instead.*" Karen grabbed her purse and stood. "Just forget it." Took a long final pull on her cigarette. "But I deserve an apology for that waiter's rudeness." She ground the butt into the plate of risotto and then stalked from the restaurant.

The owner slapped her palm to her breast. "*Che carogna!*" She flapped her hands as if scattering cockroaches. "*Fuori da qui.*"

But Paul couldn't disagree with her assessment of Karen. "*Mi dispiace, mi . . .*" He didn't know what else he could say. Had to agree, Karen could be a real bitch. "I'd like . . . *vorrei mangiare.*" He really wanted to finish his risotto. But the penance of the next six weeks was quickly descending into a deeper circle of hell. "*Mi dispiace.*"

"*Andare inseguire il suo.*" She smirked at him. "*Ragazzo.*"

"*Vorrei andare.*" Paul knew he should leave, but he didn't want her to think he needed to chase after Karen. He reached for his wallet, but the woman frowned and held out her hand, palm in his face.

"*Un altro insulto.*"

"*Mi dis—*"

"*Vi sarà un mammone per lei.*" She took up his plate. "*Deciditi, stupido.*" Headed for the kitchen.

Mammone. For God's sake, a mama's boy to Karen? "I'm so sorry." Paul wondered how long he would pay for that hour in Lindau, for his hesitations there. But he did find again the dark gaze from the kitchen door, another brief smile, and then her mother herded the girl into the kitchen. *Mammone.*

◆◆◆◆◆

In the first wash of dawn early the next morning, the walls and roofs and shutters of Varenna's houses and albergos hinted at their stunning array, the scrim of gray light barely muting their passions. A slight breeze confirmed the ancient smells of all seas and lakes, that sharp tang of a hidden and foreign life. Paul stretched, bending forward, one leg perched along the railing in front the Albergo Olivedo at the water's edge. Maybe his last single room of their tour, and it had gone to waste. So far, anyway. *Risotto al pepe verde.*

Across Lago di Como, the mountains awakened and defined themselves, rounded peak after gray peak ascending into the west like flats on a stage. He'd have to ask some local the names of those sensual shapes.

He stretched his other leg, knelt to retie his new Adidas Vienna's, and then jogged past the albergo and up the steep hill. Past the Albergo Beretta with its fawn and white striped awnings, its balconies wrapping the corner of the Viale dei Giardini, its loggia with pale red tablecloths crossed with huge and unreadable cursive scrawled in deeper scarlet by the hand of some massive roman god. And the room where Karen perhaps still dreamed of green peppers. After all, she hadn't answered his phone calls. Shit. Maybe he should have worried whether she'd made it back to her hotel safely with all those horny Italians wandering around, looking for an ass to pinch. But with rehearsal at two and the open-air concert at six, he'd find out eventually. Her own fault, then.

Once he'd run twenty minutes out from Varenna, Paul turned and headed back toward the center of town. Toward the church of San Giorgio on the piazza, and toward the Vecchia Varenna Ristorante. The narrow main street rose up a gentle slope, past buildings stuccoed and shuttered in even more shades of tangerine and lime, a rare gap between them granting now and then a tease of the long view across the slate blue water. After another half mile, the asphalt yielded to brick pavers in an ancient herringbone pattern, and Paul began to tire from the climb. He tried to picture the ristorante and how much farther it might be. And whether it would be a good idea to show himself there.

Push it, he figured. Nothing better to do this morning with Karen in such a funk. How long had he debated how to end it with her? The stubbornness, the willful pride. Her cigarettes. And yet. That fire, the way she roused their *Sturm und Drang,* and her quiet humming, after. Or simply when she'd smile and her eyes could still sink him? Couldn't they? That first day of rehearsal, two years back, when he'd looked up from the podium and she'd been watching him, didn't look away. Then that smile. Shit. Could he still feel it or was it just a lingering overtone? But her love of his music, her genuine enthusiasm for his string quartet. Wait till she saw the third movement. Once he finished.

Yeah, probably best to push it. Stick with her through the tour, try to make the best of their time in Europe, and see what the autumn brought.

But he'd write that Julia after all. That single kiss as the moon slipped into eclipse the other night in Lindau. That stunning blonde hair, her long fingers as she tucked a strand behind her ear, that lithe walk she had. He wondered what she'd be like. Let Karen pursue him this time. *Mammone.* No fucking way.

Paul reached the top of the climb and eased off as the street leveled and began a gentle descent. The stone tower of San Giorgio came into view, with the piazza at its feet. Another half mile or so.

When he reached the piazza, it was crowded with the stalls and carts of a farmers' market, white peaches and oranges and zucchini and fava beans in mounds, and breads of all shapes and sizes, crusted in hard golden shells. Tourists, recently disgorged from the Americanized Hotel Victoria, dressed in mismatched seersucker and plaids, cameras slung around their necks, strolled and gawked and, speaking English very, very slowly, slowly and emphatically, in raised voices as if addressing the deaf, handed over their lire at the stalls with the gaudiest plaques and belt buckles and painted dishes confirming their brief stay in the real life Varenna, *la Perla del* Lago di Como. He stopped in the shade from one of those trees that looked like broccoli sprouts perched on an eagle's talons and looked at his watch. Pulled up his tee shirt and wiped the sweat from his face. Close to six miles, maybe.

Here and there, strands of legato Italian drifted across the piazza as the villagers laughed with their friends, argued and negotiated and purchased the ingredients for their daily meals. Paul wandered the stalls, smiling and nodding through the crowd, wondering for a moment how this might feel as true home. Waiting for an opening between bodies, he reached across a cart to pull a bottle of aranciata from a tub of ice. At the same instant, someone else grabbed for a zucchini vined with brilliant orange blossoms. Their elbows jolted and the aranciata and zucchini leapt to the pavers. The glass shattered and the zucchini bounced and rolled.

The vendor grabbed a broom, scolding and laughing, to tidy up the glass and contain the sparkling orange liquid. Paul trotted after the zucchini and grabbed it, then turned. "Mi dispiace." He held the zucchini, its flowers soaked and dripping aranciata, and found himself face to face with the dark eyed young girl from the ristorante. "Sorry."

She took the zucchini, laughed and wiped at the aranciata, then sucked the wetness from two fingers. "Grazie."

"*Come ti chiami?*" Paul wiped his hands on his running shorts, "Your name. Do you speak English?"

"Of course," she smiled at him, "and so does Mama—fairly well, anyway."

"Hey, I'm really . . . " he looked around the piazza. "That was awful last night, I'm still embarrassed."

"I hope you didn't chase her after."

She might even be seventeen. "No, I," going on eighteen? "No." Her dark hair and eyes reminded him of another, someone from a famous painting, maybe. "I haven't seen her since then."

"*Bene*. You deserve better." She winked at him and reached out and touched his arm, giggled, and bounced on her toes. "*Il mio nome è Stefania. E tu, come ti chiami?*"

Good lord. So maybe only fifteen after all. "It's Paul. I'm Paul."

"Do you come back tonight?"

"Jeez, I don't know if your mom would—"

"*Cosa diavolo sta facendo?*" Her mother, dark eyes flashing, hair up and wound about her head in a loose bun, grabbed Stefania's shoulders and whirled her around and clutched her as if to shield her from Satan incarnate. The zucchini fell again to the pavers.

"*Mi dis*—I'm so sorry." Paul reached down for the zucchini, held it out toward them. "Madam."

"Madam? *Un altro insulto.*" She hissed into her daughter's ear, struggling with the stuffed market bag at her shoulder, and then gave Stefania a smack on the rear, sending her off across the piazza.

No look back at them.

"Look, I know you speak English, and Stefania did nothing wrong here, and I—"

"*Zitto.*" She took the zucchini. "Hush." Turned it over and rubbed one of the blossoms between her thumb and fingers. "Yes, I do speak your English, and can know what you were saying to my daughter. Trying to lie on your girl already?"

"'Cheat' is actually the word." Shit.

"*Sí.* That." She plucked off a blossom and held it to her nose, closed her eyes. "Not that she doesn't earn it."

"Deserve. But I haven't done—"

"And not with Stefania you won't."

"No, no, of course, I didn't—"

"*Silenzio.* But that *carogna* does deserve it. Hold this." She shoved the aranciata soaked zucchini at him and took his arm and led him between the tourists back to the cart where she fired a blaze of questions at the farmer. "*Bene, perfetto.*" She handed Paul a dozen zucchini, their vines still attached and wound with the tiny orange blossoms. "*Mi segua.*"

He followed her through the growing crowd, his arms loaded with the zucchini, and then down a narrowing side lane where he might have touched the stucco of the buildings on both sides if his hands were free. Struggling to keep up, he hurried after her, down into another alley, narrower still and lined with empty cartons and barrels, the cobbles uneven and buckled with the centuries. At last she opened a yellow painted door and entered the kitchen of her ristorante.

"*Grazie.*" She put the market bag on a rough wooden table and turned to reach for the zucchini. "*Risotto ai fiori di zucca al prosecco* tonight." She kissed the tips of her fingers and smiled. "A few dishes enough only."

"Are they still in season?" Paul ducked under the hanging copper pots above the table.

"*Sí.* Late, *forse* the last ones, but these are fine, silly *ragazzo.*" She squeezed next to the table and leaned into him as she plucked the zucchini from his cradling arms, her breasts against his shoulder again and again. "*Perfetto.*"

"*Perfetto, sí.*" Paul glanced down, grinned at her.

"*Ragazzo ridicolo.*" She laughed.

"What's your name?"

"Floria. And I don't want to know yours, you silly boy." She took the last few zucchini and arranged them on the table as if composing a puzzle.

"Floria?" He plucked one of the zucchini blossoms and peered at it. "*Recondita armonia,*" he half sang the words, wondering at his fantasy that all Italians would have every note of Puccini memorized. "*É bruna Floria, l'ardente amante mia.*"

She laughed again and took his blossom, one finger poised in the air. "Your name is then Cavaradossi?" Rolled the orange flower between her fingers, delicately, then opened her palm and offered the blossom for Paul to smell, the heel of her hand just off his lips. "But I won't to fly off a castle wall for you."

"Leap." He closed his eyes and tried to find names for the harmonics of the aromas her fingers had released. Fresh cut hay, perhaps, or the cork from a bottle of Valpolicella, even musk. "Yes, call me Cavaradossi." Not a fantasy, then.

"You have not his *coraggio,*" she tickled the blossom at his nose and he startled back. "*Solo l'indecisione.*"

"Maybe."

"*Forse?* There, you see?" She crossed behind him, both hands on his shoulders briefly as she squeezed by the table.

"Can't make out your mind."

"Up." Paul wondered if Stefania was in the dining room.

"*Grazie,* Cavaradossi." Floria pulled on a long apron, one of those like his grandmothers still wore but with a gigantic paisley in fluorescing oranges and chartreuses, a loop around the neck making a bib, and then drew out a paring knife from the block on the counter. She grabbed the first zucchini and laid it on a cutting board. Once she'd cut off the vines, she counted the blossoms and nodded. "Six or seven dishes enough. *Bene.*"

"I'd love to try one."

"*Sì.* Will you tonight again come?"

Paul tried to imagine the next six weeks. "We—I—play in the Oberlin Conservatory Chamber Orchestra. I'm the assistant conductor, too, so I conduct one of the pieces. We perform this evening at the piazza. Can you come? It's at eighteen—"

"I hold a *ristorante,* I cook, silly *ragazzo.*"

"Have."

She grabbed one of the zucchini and chopped it into tiny cubes. "So, you come after your concert and tell me?"

"I'm not sure—"

"*Mamonne.*" Floria slapped the knife onto the table and turned to him. "*Esci.*" She pointed to the door just as it opened. Stefania hurried in and dumped her own market basket on the table, ran her fingers through tangled hair.

Another exchange in heated Italian flew beyond Paul's abilities. Stefania tried to look at him around her mother, but Floria turned to him and shoved him out the door. "*Fuori.*" Smacked him on his ass. "Go."

Paul backed into the alley and briefly found Stefania's smile, those glowing eyes, just as the door slammed.

◆◆◆◆◆

Alone, Paul found himself wandering the slanting lanes of Varenna through the rest of the morning, looking for Karen.

Alone, through a solitary lunch of crusty bread and oil on a waterside bench, staring out across the lake, tracing absently the sensual curves of the mountains, wondering at opportunities missed in Lindau, reading and rereading the note from Julia, folding it again and again, and jamming it into his jeans' pocket. Alone, after an hour's practice—a plodding run through the Enescu *Concertstuck for Viola*—and a fitful nap in his stifling room, at last then at a secluded table in a shaded corner on the loggia of the Albergo Beretta, hovering his pencil over the shifting quicksand of the third movement of his doctoral string quartet an hour before that afternoon's rehearsal.

Paul took a sip of his tepid Perrier, swallowed its flatness. Flipped open one of the latches on his viola case, pressed it closed again. Karen had to come out of her room eventually. But would she forgive him?

She had so many times before, and it could be so sweet. He would go to her, yes, and take her in his arms, whisper something lovely and sexy and find her smile again.

He sighed and drew out the note again, its paper going tissue already after less than two days. Her scent of patchouli only a memory. *Verklarte Nacht*, indeed. Her name and address, and she'd signed it *love, Julia.* A single kiss and off she'd gone. Hadn't even found a way to make it to their performance. Out with her boyfriend, of course. Not much of a transfiguration. Maybe he should find that poem and read it to see what she'd meant.

Paul checked his watch. Just over half an hour till rehearsal, he couldn't wait much longer.

Karen truly loved him, didn't she, and yet he'd chased after that Julia like he was some slobbering puppy on a fucking leash. And for nothing. No more, then.

He crushed the note in his fist and shook it as if it were a pair of dice. Turned in his seat and cocked his arm to toss the thing over the loggia's railing.

"Come on, Mitch, stop it." Karen's voice rode a laugh from just inside the Beretta's doorway. "I mean it, now, I really do." In a tone that clearly didn't.

The door swung open and Mitch stepped out, holding it open with his violin case, and Karen followed, a look in her eyes Paul thought he recognized. Mitch? The bastard had been sniffing after Karen for a year, ever since he'd made the grad program in violin and won first chair. But she couldn't stand him.

Could she?

Paul started to get up and call her name, but found himself held fast, silent. He lowered his hand, the note held tightly, and stilled his breathing, pressed himself back into his chair, into the shadows.

"Sure you do." Mitch grinned at her and they trotted down the porch steps. "Right on." They didn't look his way.

Karen handed Mitch her oboe case and dug in her purse to find a cigarette. He put her case under his arm and reached into her bag to pluck out a book of matches, waited as she shook out the pack. Then he lit her cigarette, cupping his palms to shield a nonexistent breeze. Did his fingers touch her cheek? She withdrew the cigarette and leaned back, tilted her face upward, exhaled a long sigh of thin smoke. They both chuckled and headed off up the street.

When would she quit the fucking cigarettes?

Somehow, Paul eventually found himself at the Piazza San Giorgio, no idea how he'd gotten there, lost and swept along in a fog of the dirge-like opening movement of the Schoenberg, his own *Transfigured Night* under the startling sun. Barely made it. Shit. Dr. Talon glared at him as Paul rosined his bow. Damn it, he wasn't late. Was he? He turned and leaned to see if he could catch Karen's eye, but she struggled with her reed and frowned.

Across the piazza, the stalls had been cleared and a handful of people stood chatting or sat on the benches, tossing pistachios to the pigeons, whiling away the brilliant afternoon. The clack of a bocce ball striking its target brought a quiet cheer from a pair of white haired men in suspenders who toasted each other with tumblers of dark table wine.

"Let's start with the Schubert, we need to clean up a couple of spots." Dr. Talon tapped his baton on his stand, his jowls already dripping sweat. "Paul, if you please, opening of three, the *allegro vivace*, I'd like your gallop to be a tad lighter and quicker."

Fuck. Why hadn't he said anything yesterday?

"Sounded more like a drunken mule in Lindau." Dr. Talon grinned and pantomimed for the violin section, his girth making him almost seem clever.

A few dutiful chuckles, and Mitch laughed a bit too loud. Talon stepped off the podium and waited.

Paul lifted the needle from his Schoenberg and tried to lighten himself for the Schubert. By the time he'd stowed his viola and grabbed his own baton, he could feel his cheeks flooding. An itch at his armpits.

He flipped through the score to find the opening of the third movement, tapped his baton, raised his arms, forced a smile. Tried to find the right tempo. Karen seemed entranced in her own score, wouldn't look up. "Third movement, let's dance it, ladies and gents." Still no look. "No drunken donkeys."

"Mules." Mitch grinned up at him from his concertmaster's chair.

"Fuck you." Paul whispered, hesitating, his arms drooping a bit, still seeking entry.

From behind him, across the open piazza, a single bystander's applause. Some foolish American tourist, no doubt, who never knew when to clap and when to listen. Karen's frown deepened. Mitch laughed again as he looked beyond Paul.

The applause grew louder and Paul spun around, ready to skewer the unwashed cracker.

But there was no one in madras pants and a white belt, no one with a fifties hairstyle. A few people turned and smiled. And there she was. Stefania, poised in the opening to the narrow lane that led to the back door of the ristorante. She clapped and raised her hands higher, bounced on her toes.

Another couple, sitting on a bench near her, joined in. From the other side of the piazza, the bocce players laughed and applauded. One of them shouted *"É ora di suonare!"*

Paul raised his hands, palms out. Then took a slight bow and gave a nod to Stefania. Maybe eighteen, after all.

She waved and laughed, then disappeared into the alley.

Paul turned again to the orchestra, hummed and smiled the perfect *vivace* and conducted the Schubert with a graceful lilt. Dr. Talon would surely approve. Even Mitch and the violins seemed to find their way toward delight. But Karen, damn her, not a glance, not even when he gave her a cue for a solo passage, not even for the *rubato*.

Dr. Talon nodded him a bravo when they completed the movement, no plodding jackasses, and Paul couldn't suppress a grin as he wiped the sweat from his face. Karen sucked on a new reed.

Paul turned and scanned the piazza and found the pace slowed, the heat bristling. The afternoon sun overexposed the stonework of the surrounding buildings, grayed the dusted pavers, quieted even the pigeons. The orchestra began to wilt and Dr. Talon led them through the Schoenberg only marking, touching up transitions, molding a phrase, and here and there smearing an extra dollop of his favored Brahms over the master of twelve-tone. Paul avoided glancing Karen's direction. Focused on his viola parts, tried not to think of blonde cellists, of dark eyed teenagers and *aranciata*. Of Karen most of all.

◆ ◆ ◆ ◆ ◆

The concert that evening went well, or so Paul thought as he wandered the darkened streets of Varenna. A slight breeze filtered off the Lago di Como and he stopped for a moment across the street from the Albergo Beretta for the third time since the performance. Dr. Talon's timing, as usual, had been impeccable and he'd snared Paul, before he could seek Karen, to introduce him to the mayor of the commune. And the managing council. And, it seemed, every distant cousin and uncle and grandmother of them all. The mayor had loved the Schubert and labored out in a combination of English and Italian a drama of his music studies after the war.

"*Grazie*," Paul had smiled and nodded, "*grazie mille*." He'd been drawn along with Talon down the piazza to some ristorante, toasted repeatedly through course after course, had at last joined in rounds of the classic Italian art songs, singing verse after verse. Finally, one of the older men stood, plucked at his suspenders, closed his eyes, and sang the opening lines of *Recondita Armonia*, Cavaradossi's first aria from *Tosca*. When he soared out "*É bruna Floria, l'ardente amante mia*," Paul gripped the table and sang along. He stood and, arms around each other's shoulders, joined his new comrade, their voices both alike in their reediness, no opera singers, needing to transpose the key lower at least a couple of times as they sang of their ardent love. The aunts and uncles shouted and clapped and Paul, rubbing at his stomach, had yawned magnificently, had begged his leave.

During his three circuits around the village, Paul had turned down each pavered lane, stopped to dig a pebble from his Weejuns, to check that his shirt hadn't come unbuttoned, or to confirm his pockets still held his wad of lira, delaying outside each of the many *ristoranti*, a sidelong inspection of the diners through the glowing windows. No Karen. And no Mitch.

At the Vecchia Varrena, he stood, no pretense, watching again through the front window as Stefania made her rounds, pouring water, fetching an azure napkin, casting her glittering smile. Once only, she giggled at something and bounced on her toes before she turned and disappeared into the kitchen. Paul fingered the note in his pocket and moved on.

Last chance, he told himself. He watched the loggia of the Albergo Beretta from across the street, between a pair of those nameless trees. Last chance for you, Karen. San Giorgio chimed out eleven reminders of the hour.

"I need to get to bed, Mitch. Thanks for dinner."

Paul slipped behind one of the trees, its spiraling bark silky under his palms.

Karen crossed the intersection and headed for the steps to the loggia. Mitch tried to pat her ass and she skipped aside, slapped at his hand. But she laughed and said no more.

Paul dug his nails into the bark.

Mitch leaned close to her and said something Paul couldn't catch.

"I told you no."

As they reached the steps, Mitch grabbed Karen's hand, spun her and drew her into the shadows. He pulled her to him and kissed her. At first, she seemed to resist, but made no sound. Then her arms tightened around his neck and Paul turned away.

◆◆◆◆◆

The door was locked and lights were out at the Vecchia Varenna Ristorante, except for the glow from the kitchen door at the far end of the dining room. Paul ran his fingers through his hair, paced a few times and hummed the tune. *Recondita armonia.* He retraced his steps to the piazza and found the lane that descended to the alley and the kitchen door. Why not? Last chance, indeed. Tomorrow, to Milan and south.

As he found his way toward the back door, stumbling only a couple times in the dark, Paul tried to recall amorous lines in Italian. *Ti amo?* Sexy? There, the light spilled from a pair of windows at the kitchen.

The door opened and Paul withdrew into the shadows among the stacks of crates.

Stefania.

"*Domani*, Mama." She called and shut the door.

Paul took a deep breath, considered clearing his throat so he wouldn't startle her. He swallowed and hesitated.

"*Ti amo, piccolo mia.*" A quiet voice, from the other side of the door, and a young man stepped into the light from the kitchen. Stefania giggled and trotted to him. They kissed and then turned and walked, hand in hand, the opposite way down the alley, her head tucked into his shoulder.

Paul leaned back against the crates.

And then he heard it. Faint at first, and definitely off key, but no mistake. He mouthed the words through his grin, "*L'ardente amante mia.*"

He ran his fingers through his hair once more and stepped to the kitchen door. Tried the latch and opened it.

Floria stood with her back to him, on the other side of the worktable, pulling the apron's loop over her head, still humming the aria. She unpinned her hair and let it fall down her back, its darkness uncoiling as it drifted.

"Stefania?" Without turning, she stacked a last few plates and rambled on in Italian.

"Cavaradossi."

She lowered a final plate, sliding it gently into place, then turned, frowning. "No *coraggio*, but?" With her hair down, still crinkled from its confinement, tracing the run of buttons down her breast, she looked again the lovely archetype of classic Italian womanhood, some renaissance painting.

"Though." Paul stepped into the kitchen. "*Coraggio, sí.* I'm here."

"Too late." She smiled at last. "Though. How was your concert?"

"*Bene.* How was your risotto?"

"Another missed for you." She stepped around the table, came to him, poked him in the chest. "You still can't make out your mind. And don't fix me."

"Correct you."

"And it's '*bello*' not '*bene.*'" Floria poked him in the chest again and squeezed past him to the refrigerator. "Can you make your mind?" She opened the fridge and grabbed a flat bowl, uncovered it, held it to him as if presenting a crown on a pillow.

"*Sí.*" He moved to smell the risotto but she drew it away, touched it with the tip of her little finger and stirred, then tasted.

"*Che spreco.*" She shook her head, spooned the risotto out into a shallow pan at the stove. "Too old, too dry. *Vecchio*, not perfect. Get a prosecco from the cooler."

Paul fetched the bottle and opened it and the cork flew and the bubbles foamed out.

Floria grabbed a towel and took the bottle, wiped its sides, then licked to capture the still foaming top. "No control yourself, silly *ragazzo*. Have you Americans learn nothing?"

"Maybe." Paul reached for the bottle but she turned and poured out a bit into the risotto before handing it to him without looking his way.

"*Forse.* Maybe all you say is *forse.*"

"*Forse.*"

Floria laughed and handed him a pair of tumblers, nodded at the prosecco. "*Deciditi, mio* silly *ragazzo.*" Stirred and adjusted the flame, then sampled it again. "*Non perfetto*, too old, but you can taste if you like it."

"Yes, I think I'd like that." He poured and handed her a glass across the table.

"Think?" She stirred as the heat came up and Paul squeezed around the table to the stove, stood beside her. "*Deciditi*, Cavaradossi." She glanced at him, a smile in her eyes as she clinked her tumbler to his, slowly, gently.

"*Sí.*" Paul held her gaze, drank, and then dipped his little finger into the risotto. "*Sí.*"

◆ ◆ ◆ ◆ ◆

"It happens." Her quiet laugh like the purring of a cat.

"Not to me."

"Silly *ragazzo*." A wind chime sounded, a single tone, deep, in a wisp of breeze off the lake.

"I'm sorry."

"You still care for her, no?"

"No."

Again, a soft murmur in the darkness. "You're too quick."

"I really am sorry, that's not. . . . it wasn't you, you're stunning, *perfetto*, you're," he tried to think of the Italian for sexy.

"*Vecchia.*" She shifted onto her side, looking at him, a smile. "But that's not what I meaned: Your answer."

"Meant." He watched her.

"Fix yourself, not me. So, what is her name?"

"Karen."

"If you do care, *stupido*, can you believe why?"

"I just don't know."

"You need to remember." She rose from the bed, pulling the sheet across her breasts, her hair over one shoulder. "What made you to see her?"

"Her smile. Her eyes?" One hand brushing back long chestnut hair, the tilt of her chin, a quick glance away. Yes. "A lift of her shoulder."

"*La porcheria.*"

"No, I really—"

"*Finito.*"

"It's not bullshit, I . . . "

"*Deciditi, ragazzo mio stupido.* You need to go."

"I'm so sorry."

"*Esci.*" At the window, she turned and motioned for him to leave, as if shooing a puppy, gently, with one hand, then looked out across the water. "Go." The moonlight grazed her shoulder blades, her back, the wide flare of her naked hip. "*Deciditi.*"

Beyond her, Paul could see the moonlight on the far shore, the full moon again, the outline of the mountains fading into the distance. That single kiss.

Did he really still care? And that bastard, Mitch. Was Karen just making some point?

"*Esci.*"

"*Mi dispiace.*" He sat up and reached for his shirt.

The quiet laugh again. "You're not sorry."

Paul smiled in the darkness and pulled on his jeans.

"You're never sorry, are you, *povero ragazzo?*"

He slid his fingers into his pocket as the breeze carried her scent to him, imagined the moonlight spreading across the water. Touched again the note from Julia.

But one day, maybe?

The wind chime sounded again.

Forse.

Michael Bloom is a writer and musician, an artistic storyteller whose poetic voice sings through his fiction, poetry and songwriting. Author of two novels, short stories and children's books, Michael has been a news analyst for the Digital Music News and editor for the Fifth Wheel. He has studied with bestselling novelist Elizabeth George, author Marilyn Wallace, editor, author and educator Constance Hale, and story guru Robert McKee. He has served as a board member for the Indiana Writers Center in Indianapolis and is a co-founder of Random Acts Books, an independent collaborative publishing platform. Current projects include a novel in progress, *One Bright Day*, a time travel thriller and a short story for the upcoming *Warped, A Speculative Trio*. Michael lives in Santa Fe, New Mexico, in an adobe tucked in the foothills of the Sangre de Cristo Mountains with his wife, author Lisa Arthur, and their cat, Tiki.

www.michaelbloom.com

George H. Evans is a writer by vocation and a marketer by profession. A graduate of the fiction writing program at the University of Pittsburgh, he was greatly influenced by the work of Raymond Carver, John Cheever and Ernest Hemingway and owes what little ability he possesses to the words and mentorship of Monty Culver and the outlaw Chuck Kinder. Like the poet Evan Shipman, George chose his career path as a "matter of substance," but has been writing short fiction as a matter of therapy for more than thirty-five years. George is the author of the collection *Buffalo & Rochelle* and a co-author of the anthology *Lobster Tales*. He also has two screenplays in circulation that are a constant source of frustration and anti-establishment anger. George is a member of the Indiana Writers Center as well as a founding member of Random Acts Books and The Loose Lobsters Writers' Project.

David M. Hassler is a long-time member of the Indiana Writers Center Faculty and he holds an MFA from Spalding University. His award winning work has been published in journals including Maize and the Santa Fe Writers' Project. He served as Student Editor for *The Louisville Review* and as Technical Editor for *Writing Fiction for Dummies*. He is currently Managing Editor for *Flying Island* and blogs at *The Write Current*. Future projects include an historical novel of the Civil War, *To Strike a Single Hour*, which seeks to find truth in one of P T Barnum's heroic creations, due out in 2015; *A Distant Polyphony*, a collection of linked stories about music and love, memories and loss, due out in 2016; and a science fiction novelette, *And on the Eighth Day, A Tale of the Last Time Traveler*, due out in…well, since it's a time travel story, it really doesn't matter.